Lisa Ann

Enchanted Pony Academy

Let It Glow

SCHOLASTIC

To my husband, Patrick,
who always helps me make
writing a priority.
Love you!

· Chapter One ·

Electra shuffled her hooves and glanced out the window as she waited for history class to finish.

"What's wrong?" her friend Daisy asked quietly as the teacher passed back their quiz papers.

Electra always had trouble standing still in history class. She'd much rather be outside running through the fields at the Enchanted Pony Academy. Her outdoor classes, like weather casting, were great. She hated being stuck inside. But today, being cooped up in class was even worse. Today was an extra-special day.

"I'm just excited!" Electra whispered. "Riding lessons start in a few minutes."

"You'll be great. Probably the best in the class!" Daisy said.

Electra smiled. "I sure hope so!"

The school bell rang, and Electra bolted out the door. She had enough time for a quick run along the apple orchard before she had to be at the stables to gear up for riding class.

Electra loved nothing more than running as fast as she could, the wind whipping through her mane. Charging through the fields, her magical hooves left behind a cloud of glitter. No other pony at school could keep up with her. Back home, the other ponies gave up trying to beat her a long time ago. If she weren't a Glitter Pony,

destined to be paired up with a royal child, she definitely would've wanted to become a race horse.

But Electra was very excited to find her perfect match among the royal children, and she was certain her running skills would help. She didn't have the top grades among the first-year ponies. She didn't have the best Glitter Gift, either. Daisy could turn invisible! Her pegapony friend, Skydancer, could talk to winged creatures. All Electra could do was make her horn and hooves glow. Sometimes, they glowed on their own when she was excited. She could feel a warm tingle whenever they started to light up. It was a nice gift, but it didn't seem good enough to make a prince or princess choose her as their pet someday.

But riding? Once the children saw how fast she could go and how fun she was to ride, she hoped they'd be lining up to choose her on selection day. Then she'd hopefully find her perfect royal companion. Together, they'd help rule a kingdom. And today, she'd get to work with those children for the first time! She reared up in excitement.

Electra snatched an apple off the tree and munched on her snack as she galloped to the riding stables.

This is going to be the best day ever, she thought. *Everyone is going to want to ride with me.*

· · Chapter Two · ·

Electra hurried to join the first-year ponies on the field, along with the lead ponies

from each of the barns. Rasha, the lead pony from the Sky barn, greeted her. "Can't wait to see you ride!"

Electra pranced in place, eager to get started. "I can't wait, either!"

"This is so exciting!" said her friend Razzle. "It'll be so much fun working with the children."

"Woo-hoo!" shouted their classmate Stone, who shot a stream of sparks from

his horn. That was his Glitter Gift, and he used it all the time.

"I'm a little nervous," Daisy said. "I've never ridden with someone on my back."

Razzle giggled. "Of course not, silly. No one's allowed to ride a Glitter Pony until they come to the academy."

"We can prance and trot and gallop!" Skydancer exclaimed. "It'll be a blast. I wonder when I get to fly with the children?" She flapped her shiny white wings.

Electra smiled, happy all her friends were excited, too. Hopefully, they didn't feel bad that they weren't as fast as she was.

Mulligan, the old pony who was equipment keeper for the school, whinnied loudly to get everyone's attention. "Welcome, ponies, to your very first riding class. This is an introductory course, so don't worry, it'll be nice and easy. And how's this for exciting? Soon, you'll work with a designer to create your own special saddle. But for now, the school's training saddles will do. Let's get you geared up!"

Buckles clinked and leather squeaked as the ponies were suited up with saddles.

When it was Electra's turn, Mulligan levitated the saddle on to her back and tightened the straps around her. Next came the bridle and harness. It all felt bulky and tight. She'd never had riding gear on before.

She wriggled and swatted her tail around. She hadn't expected it to be so uncomfortable.

"Don't worry, lassie, you'll be fine," Mulligan said.

"Oh, I know. I'm just getting used to it," she said.

The other students were giggling and

rearing, teasing each other while showing off their gear.

"Aren't these saddles neat?" Razzle asked.

"Sure," Electra said, not caring one bit what they looked like. "I just can't wait to ride." Once she was out on the field racing away, she wouldn't even notice the saddle.

When everyone was ready, Electra led the group to the training field, running with all her might.

As they arrived at the field, she spotted a group of children waiting for them. They waved and smiled and stood on their toes for a better look. Some wore their royal crowns and capes. One pretty girl with long red braids sat in a chair with wheels. Electra had never seen such a thing.

A few of the children were pointing at Electra. "I want to ride that unipony!" said one girl.

"Look at her colours! She's got a rainbow mane!" said another.

Electra was so excited that she kicked out her back legs.

Now all of the children were watching her with wide eyes. She neighed excitedly. This was going to be so much fun.

"Welcome, royal children," said Professor Wallina, the academy's riding teacher. "It is time to start working with our ponies so you both can perfect the art of riding. Then when your selection day comes, you'll be ready to ride off with the new pet you choose in our celebration ceremony."

The ponies whinnied, and the children cheered.

She continued. "Ponies, of all your classes, this is one of the most important. You must pass this beginner class before you can move on to the more advanced riding classes. And you won't be included in the selection ceremony until you pass all your riding classes. Glitter Ponies must be able to ride with their royal children."

No problem, thought Electra, champing at the bit to get started.

A man in tall boots and a hat stepped forward. "Hello, everyone. I'm Professor Maximus, a riding instructor from the Royal Children's Academy. We have two weeks to work with the ponies and pass this introductory course before you return to your kingdoms. This is also a good opportunity to get to know the ponies that will be included in your selection ceremony next year."

Electra got goose bumps just thinking about that special day. How wonderful it would be to find her perfect royal match. She couldn't wait!

The teacher continued. "Children, choose a pony, and I'll instruct you how to mount."

The ponies pranced in place and bobbed their heads in excitement as the group of children headed towards them.

"I want to ride a unipony!" cried one girl.

"Me too!" said another, quickly grabbing Violet's reins. Violet was delighted.

There were only a few uniponies among the first-year students, and several children were running towards Electra. Excited, she reared up and whinnied. The girls stopped and screeched.

"That unipony is wild!" said one of the girls, backing away and tripping.

"I'm not riding that unipony," said a girl.

"Me neither!" said another. "I'm too scared!"

Suddenly, all the children were running *away* from Electra.

"No! Don't be scared of me. I'm not wild. I'm just excited," Electra said, a bit embarrassed.

Still, the children looked at her cautiously. Then they turned to the other ponies, each choosing the one with whom they wanted to ride.

No one's picking me! she thought nervously. *I'll show them what I can do.* She turned and ran a few fast circles around the field so they could see how much fun she'd be, then returned to the group of remaining students.

"You're really fast," said one boy, sounding worried instead of impressed.

"I'm too scared to try that unipony," said a girl who scampered over to Daisy for a ride.

Soon, only a few children were left who hadn't picked a pony yet, including the girl in the chair. And she was reading a book, paying no attention at all to the ponies.

Electra gulped. Was no one going to choose her? She pawed at the ground.

Then a tall boy puffed out his chest and walked in her direction. "I can ride with her."

⋆ Chapter Three ⋆·

Electra smiled, relieved she was going to get to show off what she could do.

The boy took hold of her reins and led her to the centre of the field.

Electra couldn't wait to ride. "What's your name?" she asked him.

"Prince Dmitri." He stepped into the stirrups.

Electra grunted as he sat on her back. He was heavier than she expected. Then he yanked the reins and nudged her in the ribs. "Ride!" he commanded.

Surprised by his tone, she tore across the field. But she couldn't run as fast as usual. The boy on her back was slowing her down. She didn't like that feeling. Gathering all her strength, she sped forward.

Prince Dmitri pulled on her reins. Startled by the unfamiliar feeling, she bucked her back legs. But he held on, tugging harder.

Is this really how riding works? she wondered.

"Stop!" he hollered.

She stopped bucking and kept running.

"Stop!" he shouted louder.

She wasn't sure what the boy wanted. It was hard getting used to following someone else's orders, but Electra came to a sudden stop. The boy flew forward, tumbling off the saddle on to the ground.

"Hey!" He glared up at her from where he was sprawled in the soft dirt. "Why did you do that?"

Electra was confused. "You told me to stop, so I did!"

He stood, dusting himself off. "You don't know anything."

Everyone had stopped to stare at Electra.

"She's not a very good pony," one child said.

"I'm never going to ride her," said another, crossing her arms.

All of the children started whispering and casting looks her way.

The girl in the chair slammed her book shut. "Excuse me," she said, tipping up her chin. "Didn't we just talk about the importance of kindness in our classes? Royal children are supposed to set a good example. Are you doing that by saying such nasty things to this nice pony?" She stared them down with icy blue eyes.

"No," said a few of the children.

"I'm sorry," said another.

Electra blinked and looked down.

The girl in the chair softened her tone. "This is new to all of us. We must be patient as we learn new skills, and treat our hosts with respect." Then the girl wheeled her chair away from the group, before Electra could say thank you for sticking up for her.

The lead ponies from the four barns

trotted over to her. "Are you OK, Electra?" asked Rasha.

Electra flicked her tail back and forth angrily. "I'm fine."

Belissima, the lead pony from the Earth barn, tossed her beautiful pink mane. "It takes some ponies a little time to get used to riding with children. You'll be fine."

Electra nodded, but she still felt sad. She'd been so certain she'd be one of the ponies who was amazing at riding. How had it gone so wrong?

"You get another chance tomorrow," Rasha said. "It'll get easier and easier each time."

I hope so, Electra thought.

"Thanks," she said to the lead ponies. "I'll see you later." Electra ran to the stables without looking back. The saddle seemed to be getting heavier and heavier, and scratchier and scratchier.

"Get this off me," Electra begged Mulligan by the time she got to the barn.

He chuckled. "Don't worry, it takes some getting used to."

Electra sighed as Mulligan charmed the riding gear off her. "I don't understand. I thought this was going to be so easy for me, but my child fell and got angry."

He nodded sympathetically. "Well, you know what they say. If someone falls off, you've got to help them get back on. You'll get the hang of it, lassie."

"I'm worried no one else is going to give me a chance."

"Of course they will. You'll get the swing of things."

"I hope so. I love running. But it's hard with a child," Electra said sadly.

"Well, I'll see you back here tomorrow, little filly. You'll have a better day. There's

always a way to work out your problems.
Don't forget that."

Chapter Four

Electra plodded on to weather casting class and couldn't concentrate on the lesson about hail. She was going to have to borrow someone's notes to study!

After classes, Electra wanted to be alone, so she settled into her stall in the Sky barn stables. She lay down in her cozy bed of clouds. She always loved looking at the beautiful decorations enchanting her room and the stars that hovered on the ceiling, but today they didn't cheer her up. She closed her eyes and drifted off to sleep.

"Electra?" Rasha stood outside her stall. "Are you feeling better?"

Electra stood and shook off her coat. "Yes. Of course." She didn't want to admit how bad she was really feeling.

"It's almost time for dinner. I heard there are sugar cubes for dessert!"

Electra nodded. "OK, let's go."

But at dinner, all the other ponies were chattering about how much fun they'd had riding with the children.

"My child gave me a carrot!" Daisy said. "It was so wonderful. She loved when I made us disappear!"

"Mine braided my tail!" Razzle said.

"I can't wait for the next class," Daisy said dreamily.

"And we can ride after classes, too!" Skydancer said. "We can work on tricks and challenges if we want to! You missed that announcement when you ran off, Electra," she explained. "What happened? Why did you leave?"

"My ride didn't go well," Electra said quietly.

"It'll be better tomorrow," Daisy said.

Well, it couldn't be worse, right? thought Electra. She was lucky to have such kind, encouraging friends. Tomorrow, she'd show them what a good riding partner she could be.

But she had bad dreams that night of children falling off and yelling at her. She tossed and turned and woke up exhausted.

Then she worried all morning long during her other classes. She kept dropping things during levitation class. She couldn't remember any of the answers for her composition test. She was getting more nervous about riding class as the day went on.

When she got to the riding field, the girl with bright red hair was sitting in her chair reading a book. She didn't look up when Electra passed.

The rest of the children shied away from her. The big boy who had ridden her had scratches on his face. He sneered. "No one's going to want that unipony for a royal companion," he said.

Electra's jaw dropped. What a hurtful thing to say!

"Prince Dmitri, that's enough," said Professor Maximus.

The prince stalked away.

While some children petted the other ponies, and offered them carrots and sugar cubes, the rest of the children stared at her with wide eyes and fearful faces. Electra had never felt so embarrassed.

A little girl wearing a big crown walked over. "I'm going to be queen someday. I can handle this Glitter Pony."

Electra wanted a second chance to prove herself, but she was worried. Would this child like her?

Chapter Five

The girl stepped into the stirrup and swung her leg over Electra. She wasn't as heavy as the boy had been. Maybe this would be easier.

"What is your name?" the girl asked.

"I'm Electra. Who are you?"

"I'm Princess Antonia, and I can't wait to ride with you!"

Electra bobbed her head. "Me too. It's my favourite thing to do."

"Let's go!"

Electra trotted across the field. She turned

in whichever direction the reins were leading her. It was an odd feeling, having someone in charge of where she was going. She wanted to trot along the apple orchard to search for fallen snacks. But the girl led her straight down the middle of the field.

It certainly wasn't as fun as riding by herself. Not being in control of where she was going wasn't the only problem. Electra was uncomfortable. She didn't like the feel

of the bit in her mouth. The saddle rubbed against her back.

The princess ruffled Electra's mane. "I love these bright colours. I definitely want a unipony for my pet. I might consider you when it's time for my selection ceremony. What is your Glitter Gift?"

"I can make my horn and hooves glow," Electra responded.

"May I see, please?"

Electra tried to make them glow, but the strong, warm feeling she usually got was much weaker. She checked a hoof, and it was just barely lit up. What was happening to her?

"That's it?" The girl sounded disappointed.

"It's usually brighter. I don't know what's wrong. Maybe it doesn't work as well when I'm riding." *Or when I'm disappointed*, she thought.

"Fine. Show me later. Right now, I want to go faster," the girl announced.

"OK," Electra said, trotting across the field. She relaxed a little as the breeze whipped through her mane.

Electra ran faster, wondering if she'd ever get used to the feeling of someone on top of her. Just as she managed to get running at full speed, the girl started screaming.

"You're going too fast! I'm scared! Stop!" the girl hollered.

This time, Electra knew to slow down before stopping so the girl wouldn't fly off.

But the girl was in tears as she climbed down. "I'm sorry, but I think I need a pony who's not so wild."

Electra blinked a few times. Wild? "I'm not wild. . ."

Every pony and child was staring at her. Again. Then they started whispering.

"I'm not going to ride that pony."

"I'm too scared!"

"She goes too fast!"

Electra's ears drooped. How had she messed up riding lessons *twice*? She was supposed to be the best in the class at this, not the worst. She wasn't supposed to be the pony no one wanted to ride.

"Children, you have some free time if you'd like to explore the school grounds," said their instructor.

"Let's go climb the apple trees!" shouted one of the girls.

"Come on, I'll race you!" said another.

Electra noticed that no one invited the redheaded girl who was reading. Electra walked over to her. "You should go with them. Our apples are delicious."

The girl looked up at her. "No one invited me. Besides, I'm not in the mood

for apples." She wheeled away from Electra towards the rose gardens lining the training field.

Electra couldn't believe it. None of the children liked her! Not even the kind girl in the chair – who couldn't even be afraid of riding her, since she hadn't been working with any of the ponies.

"Ponies, that's all for today," said Professor Wallina. "If you'd like to return after classes to work on tricks and challenges, meet here at the training field."

Skydancer raced over to Electra. "Want to come back with us later?"

"No, thanks," she said quietly. "I'll see you at dinner."

"OK. Don't let those children upset you," Skydancer said. "Soon they'll see how wonderful you are."

"I don't know," Electra said. "Maybe I just can't do this."

"Don't say that!" Daisy scolded. "Don't give up. If anyone can do it, you can. You're the best runner in our class. You'll get the hang of it."

"Thanks." Electra trudged towards her next class, each step seeming like her hooves were made of lead. She tried to light them up but felt absolutely nothing. Her heart sank. She couldn't ride with the children, and now she was losing her Glitter Gift?

Professor Wallina trotted up beside her. "Can we talk?"

Electra nodded. "Sure."

"What seems to be the problem during riding class?" the professor asked.

"I don't know. I'm not used to having a child on my back. I don't like how it feels. And they don't like when I run fast."

"Well, you have to pass this class in order to move on to the next phase. Riding lessons continue when the children return to the academy in a few months." Professor Wallina softened her voice. "You won't be included in the selection ceremony until you pass riding lessons."

Electra gulped. She wasn't sure she could even get a child to give her another chance and climb on for a ride. Maybe the children would never trust her.

"What happens if none of the children pick me during the selection ceremony?"

"Then you work at the academy," Professor Wallina said kindly. "Ponies can also decide not to be included in the ceremony. That's the choice I made." The professor looked off across the fields. "I wasn't picked in the first selection ceremony. I was so embarrassed. I wasn't brave enough to join another selection ceremony and be rejected again."

"But you like being a teacher, right?" Electra asked.

Professor Wallina smiled. "Of course. I'm very happy working at the academy with all you wonderful young ponies. It's a privilege, and I truly believe I was meant to be a teacher. But being chosen as a royal pet is a great honour, too. You don't want to miss that opportunity. There is such an incredible

bond between a pony and their child. I've
been told it's one of the best things in life.
You'll find just the right child, I'm sure.
Your one true match. If you really want it,
you'll find a way to pass riding."

"Thanks," Electra said. "You really are
a great teacher."

"What a kind thing to say, Electra. And
I have no doubt you can do anything you
set your mind to."

Electra nodded, but she wasn't sure she believed her.

Chapter Six

After classes, while the other ponies were riding with the students during their free time, Electra wandered over to the gardens. No one would notice her there. She just wanted to be alone. She understood what Professor Wallina meant when she said she didn't want to be rejected again. Her spirit was crushed knowing the children didn't want to ride her.

Electra lay among the rosebushes, keeping careful watch on the bees buzzing about. A butterfly landed on her nose, tickling her.

She sighed. It was peaceful and beautiful here, but that couldn't chase away her bad thoughts.

Even if she could pass riding lessons, would any of the children want to select her? Glitter Ponies who weren't picked after four selection ceremonies stayed to work at the school. Maybe that would happen to her.

The gardens might be a nice place to work, she thought. Her horn glowed softly at the thought. *At least that's not totally gone.*

"I like your horn," said a voice nearby.

Electra was startled. She thought she was alone, but then she noticed the girl in the chair. "I didn't see you there," Electra said, standing up.

"I'm good at hiding." The girl smiled, then wheeled her chair towards Electra.

"Can you go fast in your chair?" Electra asked.

The girl rolled her eyes. "No. But it gets me where I need to go. There are lots of things I can do with it."

"Why aren't you riding a pony?" Electra asked. "Seems like that would be even better than a wheelchair. You could go faster, at least."

The girl was quiet for a moment. "I can't sit up on my own. Someone would have to walk alongside me, holding me, and that's no fun at all. I'm never going to ride a Glitter Pony."

"But what will you do with your pony after the selection ceremony?"

"I don't know." She looked away from Electra. "It doesn't matter."

Electra felt a pain in her heart listening to the sadness in the girl's voice. "What's your name?"

"Princess Alana. What's yours?"

"I'm Electra."

"That's pretty. Why aren't you riding with the children?" Alana asked.

Electra kicked at a pebble. "You saw what happened with Prince Dmitri and then Princess Antonia. I guess I'm not very good at it. They don't want to ride me." A bee that had been buzzing around the rosebushes darted towards the princess. Electra swished her tail to shoo it away.

"Hey!" Alana cried, batting away her tail.

"I'm sorry! I was trying to keep a bee from you." Electra hung her head. She just didn't know the right way to behave around children.

"Oh, I didn't realize. That was very kind. I shouldn't have got so upset. I thought you were being mean."

Electra shook her head. "I would never

do that. I should leave you alone. I'm just not comfortable around children, I guess." That had never occurred to her. She could ace all of her classes at the academy, but there was no guarantee she could learn how to be at ease with children.

"Please don't go! I'm not comfortable around children, either," Alana said with a laugh. "Sometimes, people look at me funny because I can't walk. But I like you being here with me." She wheeled herself back to her original spot and picked up a palette of paints off a small table.

Electra noticed that the girl also had an easel with a colourful canvas propped on it. "Did you paint that?"

"Yes. I love painting. It's something I can do all by myself." It was a picture of the roses in the garden.

"It's lovely. You're quite talented."

"Thank you. I'm very good at painting things I can look at. I wish I could be a painter instead of a princess. I'd rather just travel the world by myself and paint all the beautiful things I see." Alana had a dreamy look in her eyes.

"There's an amazing river nearby with seaponies! I bet you could paint that," Electra said.

"Seaponies!" Alana's smile fell. "It's

probably too far for me in this chair."

Electra frowned. Daisy had found a path to the river for the ponies, but it was a long walk through the woods. There had to be another way to get Alana to the river, but how?

Electra and Alana watched through the rosebushes as the children and ponies continued riding. After a while, the children dismounted and headed towards the rainbow stairs to return home for the night.

"Time for me to go." Alana gathered her painting supplies onto her lap.

"Are you coming back tomorrow?" Electra asked.

"I have to," she said.

"Want to meet here after classes?"

Alana smiled. "I'd like that."

As Alana headed for the rainbow, Electra tore off through the fields, enjoying the wind whipping through her mane. She felt like she could run for hours – all by herself. It was so much more fun without a child on her back.

Princess Alana probably hasn't ever felt such a thrill, she thought sadly. Her chair certainly couldn't move that fast.

Then Electra was struck by the most wonderful idea. *I know exactly how she could feel this thrill!*

Chapter Seven

Electra ran straight to the stables to get permission for her plan.

"That's a wonderful idea!" Mulligan said. "Not sure if it'll count as riding, but I'll help you get set up. You sure are a smart one."

Electra felt proud and relieved she might have found a solution.

"I'll bring Alana here tomorrow after my classes are done," Electra said.

The next day, Electra was the last pony picked during riding class.

"Go slow!" the girl warned. "No running. I don't want to fall off."

"I will go very slowly," Electra said. "Don't worry."

Electra was walking painfully slowly across the field. She could do this. She just had to try harder.

"I'm slipping!" the girl cried.

"Hang on to the saddle," Electra told her.

"Stop walking!" the girl cried.

Electra stopped, but the girl still slid off the saddle and tumbled on to the ground in tears.

Electra hung her head, embarrassed that everyone was staring at her — yet again. Maybe she really couldn't ride with a child on her back. Maybe something was wrong with her. The thought made her very sad. But at least she had her surprise for Alana to look forward to. She could only hope

Alana was willing to give it a try.

Finally the rest of her classes were over. As the other ponies headed for the training fields for more riding, Electra charged over to the gardens.

Alana was sketching a butterfly. "Hi, Electra!" she said with a smile.

"How would you like to gallop around the track at the exhibition field?"

Alana's voice hardened. "I told you, I don't want to."

"You don't have to ride on a horse. You can always find a way when there's something you really want. Come with me and I'll explain."

Alana followed Electra to the riding stables.

Mulligan stood outside next to the glorious golden chariot used during ceremonial events at the school like Homecoming.

"You're going to ride in that!" Electra said. "And I'll pull you."

"We can lock your chair in," Mulligan said.

Electra pranced nervously in place. "Want to try? I can run really fast. It'll be fun!"

Alana bit her bottom lip. "Not too fast."

"I'll go as slow or as fast as you want," Electra said.

Alana wheeled her chair up a ramp into

the chariot while Electra was strapped into the harness. The gear was bulky, but she was excited to pull Alana around the track. Electra looked behind her. "Ready?"

"Ready!" Alana said, wide-eyed. "But remember, not too fast!"

Electra clip-clopped over to the track and started slowly circling the field.

"Woo-hoo!" Alana shouted. "I love this!"

Electra smiled and started trotting.

"Faster!"

Electra looked back at the girl. "Are you sure?"

She laughed and raised her arms into the air. "Yes!"

Electra ran faster, thrilled to hear Alana hollering in delight. Surely, this would help her pass riding lessons. Mulligan had been right. There was always a way to work things out.

After Alana left to return home, Electra ran to the headmistress's office to find out if she could pull a chariot for her riding exam.

Headmistress Valincia listened intently to Electra's tale of pulling Alana in the chariot, but then she frowned. "While that sounds incredibly wonderful and fun, it doesn't count as riding. I'm sorry. As a Glitter Pony, you must to learn to ride with a child on your back."

The happiness that had filled Electra's heart disappeared. She was so sure the chariot was the answer to all her problems. Now what? She left the headmistress's office feeling hopeless.

Chapter Eight

No children lined up to ride Electra during lessons the next day. So she munched on tiny daisies growing in the field, hoping no one could see the tears filling her eyes.

"What are you going to do?" Skydancer asked her at the end of class. "You have to learn to ride."

"I don't know," Electra said. "The children are all scared of me."

"Please cheer up." Daisy levitated an apple from the orchard and presented it to Electra, but she was too sad to eat it. She set it aside for Alana.

Electra stood on the side of the field watching the other horses easily trot back and forth with the royal children. They laughed and whooped in delight as they rode, which only made Electra feel worse.

After classes let out for the day, Electra found Alana in the garden. "I have a present for you." She levitated the apple onto her lap.

"How wonderful! You have such strong magic."

"Thanks," Electra said quietly.

"Look what I painted." Alana held up a portrait of Electra.

"Wow! That looks just like me. What an incredible job!"

Alana blushed. "You can keep it."

"I'll hang it up in my stall."

Alana sighed. "I'm sick of painting flowers. I can't stop thinking about the seaponies. Do you think we could take the chariot to see them?"

"We could try! Gather your supplies and I'll ask Daisy to come with us. She knows how to get the seaponies to rise to the surface."

Electra galloped to the training field. A

child was climbing off Daisy's back.

"You're the best pony ever!" the little girl said.

Daisy bobbed her head shyly. "Thanks."

Would any child ever say that about me? Electra wondered. She trotted over to Daisy. "Can you come visit the seaponies with me? My friend Alana wants to see them, but I'm not sure I can get them to rise to the surface."

"Sure! I love visiting Marina."

Daisy and Electra galloped back to the rose garden.

"Princess Alana, I'd like you to meet my friend Daisy."

"So nice to meet you!" Alana said. "Your coat is the same colour as the roses on one of the bushes. It's so pretty."

Dark pink circles appeared on Daisy's cheeks as she softly said, "Thank you."

"Daisy, show her your Glitter Gift!" Electra said.

Daisy stomped her hooves and disappeared.

Alana gasped then clapped.

Daisy reappeared and took a bow.

"Daisy would be a great pony to choose in the selection ceremony," Electra said. "She's so kind and nice. And all the children love riding her."

Daisy smiled. "How come I haven't seen you riding with the other children, Alana?"

"Because I can't do it. And I'd rather paint anyway," Alana said.

"But don't you want a pony someday?" Daisy asked.

Alana shrugged. "I don't really care about getting a pony."

"Every royal child needs a Glitter Pony," Daisy said.

"Why get a pony if I can't ride it?" Alana asked.

"But how will you know if you never try?" Electra asked.

Alana said nothing.

"Well, let's head to the stable and get the chariot hooked up," Electra said.

"What fun!" Daisy said.

Once Alana was secured in the chariot, they headed towards the spot in the woods that led to the river without leaving campus.

"I can't wait to see a seapony!" Alana said.

"They're so cute," Daisy said. "And very nice, too."

They galloped up to the trail in the woods that led to the river. Electra tried to pull the chariot into the woods, but it was too big. It wouldn't fit between the trees. "I'm sorry, Alana. This isn't going to work. If

only there were a way for you to ride on my back."

Alana sniffed. "It's fine. Really. I'll just draw more flowers. I like flowers."

They slowly went back to the barn. Alana didn't say a word the whole ride home.

"See you at dinner!" Daisy said, galloping off.

Electra and Alana returned to the gardens.

"I'll see you tomorrow," Electra said

quietly, disappointed she hadn't been able to help Alana.

"Electra, I have a favour to ask."

"Sure, anything."

Alana paused for a moment. "Can I try to ride you tomorrow?"

Electra could hardly believe her ears. "Really? Are you sure?"

"Maybe you were right. How will I ever know if I can ride or not if I don't try? And I wasn't telling the truth. I really want a pony for my royal pet. I really do."

"I thought you were too frustrated to try riding?" Electra asked.

"I'm not going to let that stop me. It would be a dream to ride a pony. I'm just scared that I can't do it."

"You can do it!" Electra said. "I know you can."

Alana bit her lower lip. "I thought maybe

we could try in private, over here in the rose garden?"

"Of course! I can't wait."

"Me too. But I'm nervous. What if it doesn't work?" Alana asked.

"It will."

Alana smiled. "OK. Thanks. I'll see you tomorrow!"

"Great! And don't worry – everything will be fine." Electra whinnied in delight and trotted off for a run along the apple orchards. A child actually wanted to ride her. And not just any child, but the sweetest child she'd ever met. She couldn't disappoint her.

But Electra stopped running and headed to her stall. Every single child had hated riding her so far. What if Alana did, too? What if she lost her as a friend?

Chapter Nine

The next day after classes, Mulligan geared up Electra and she trotted nervously over to the garden with Alana.

"Thank you for letting us try this over here," Alana said to Mulligan.

"You be careful," said Alana's father, who was standing on one side of Electra while one of his guards stood on the other. "I'll be walking alongside you the whole way."

Alana rolled her eyes.

The huge guard lifted Alana out of her chair and placed her on the saddle.

Electra thought Alana felt as light as a feather.

Alana giggled. "This is amazing! I can see everything up here. It's very comfortable, too. Oh, I love this!" She patted Electra's mane. "Can you please take a few steps, Electra?"

"Of course." Slowly, Electra moved forward as carefully as she could. She did not want to spook Alana.

Her father and the guard moved along with Electra as she cautiously rode into the gardens. Alana squealed in delight. It was one of the best sounds Electra had ever heard.

Electra closed her eyes, and breathed in the scent of roses. It was a bright day, and the sun warmed her coat. She didn't know she could feel so happy with a child on top of her.

And then something sharp stuck her leg. "Ow!" Surprised, she flinched trying to shake it away.

Alana shrieked, sliding off the saddle into her father's arms. Alana started crying. "I knew I couldn't do it!"

"I'm so sorry! I got stung by a bee. I was surprised!" Electra was afraid she might cry in frustration. "Please try again. I won't shake you off, I promise."

"No," Alana said through her tears. "No, I can't. I won't!"

"Please, Alana, don't be mad! I didn't mean to knock you off." *Why do all the children fall off of me? Why can't I do this right?*

Alana wiped away her tears. "I'm not mad. I'm just sad. I knew I couldn't ride. I wish I hadn't even tried. It was a dumb idea. I want to go home, Father. I don't want to come back here. Ever."

"Alana, no!" shouted Electra. "It's my fault. Maybe I'm not meant to be a royal pony. Not if I'm so bad at it."

"You don't mean that!" Alana said.

"I do. I'd be a horrible royal pony. But I'm sure you can ride. Try a different pony. A better pony."

"No," Alana said softly. "I can't." She started sobbing.

"I'm sorry this didn't work. You should return to your stable, Electra," Alana's father said.

With a heavy heart, Electra trudged back to her stall. She stayed there for the rest of the day, not even coming out for dinner.

She was dozing when a knock on her stall door awakened her. It was her friends, all looking at her with big, sad eyes.

"Electra, we're worried about you," said Daisy.

"You're so sad all the time, and you've been keeping to yourself," Razzle said. "We miss you."

"I miss seeing your horn glow. I haven't seen it glow in a long time," Skydancer said.

Electra tried to make her horn and hooves glow, but she couldn't. "I'm too sad to make it glow. I'm not going to pass Introduction to Riding."

Her friends didn't say anything.

"It doesn't matter. I'm not so sure I want to be a royal pet any more," Electra said quietly.

"Of course you do," Daisy said. "You've worked so hard. Don't give up now. You'll find a way to make things work."

"We're going to start designing our saddles tomorrow," Skydancer said. "Maybe if you make the most beautiful one ever, the children will try riding you again."

"You think?" Electra asked.

"Of course!" said Razzle. "Any child would be lucky to have you for a pet."

"Get a good night's sleep and think of some great ideas for your saddle," Daisy said. "Everything is going to be fine. The final riding exam isn't for another week. You've got time to catch up."

"Thanks," Electra said. "You guys are such good friends."

When she was alone again, Electra gazed up at the stars in her stall. Could a wonderful saddle really solve all her problems?

Chapter Ten

Since no child had chosen to ride her during class, and since she didn't see Alana in the rose garden, Electra spent the time during riding lessons drawing saddle designs with her inky quill. She'd got good at her levitation skills, and could easily draw, but that didn't mean she had many good ideas for a saddle.

She tore up design after design. There was only one child she cared about – Alana. Maybe she could design a saddle for her.

So Electra sketched out a beautiful saddle

covered in butterflies and roses. "Can we make these different colours?" she asked Mulligan when she handed in her design.

"Of course! This is one of the most unique saddles I've ever seen. I wonder what lucky child will get to use it?" he asked.

None of them, thought Electra sadly.

Her friends gathered around her and admired the picture. "That is so beautiful!" Daisy said. "Alana will love it!"

"She'll never see it. Didn't you notice, she doesn't come to class any more," Electra said.

"I can send a message for her with one of my bird friends!" Skydancer suggested.

"Really?" Electra felt a flutter of hope.

"The saddle will be ready in a week," said Mulligan.

"Excellent!" Electra said. She trotted back to her room and levitated a quill to write her message.

Dear Alana,
This week we got to design our own saddles and I made one especially for you.
I do hope you'll come back to class so you can see it. It will be ready in a week.
Please come. I miss you.

Love, Electra

Skydancer found a lovely bluebird who was willing to deliver the message to the Royal Children's Academy. It was going to be a long week waiting to see if Alana would return to school.

Electra showed up to riding class each day for the rest of the week, but none of the children would ride her. She didn't care. She only wanted one child on her back and that was

Alana. Hopefully, her saddle was beautiful enough that Alana would try one more time.

At the end of the week, Mulligan came to riding class pulling a wagon filled with saddles.

The ponies whinnied and reared in excitement as the saddles were passed out. Electra kept watching the path that led to the training field to see if Alana was coming.

Children crowded around the ponies as they were fitted with their special saddles.

"This turned out beautifully," said Mulligan as he pulled the wagon over to Electra.

The saddle was covered with roses in different shades of pink and a few butterflies in hues of yellow and blue. It was the most gorgeous thing Electra had ever seen.

"It will look lovely with your colourful

mane," Rasha said as she oversaw the ponies from her barn.

"Let's get you saddled up, lassie." Mulligan levitated the saddle on to Electra's back. For once, she didn't mind it so much.

"This fits so much better than the other saddles," Electra said.

Mulligan smiled. "That's because it's made especially for you."

The children looked at Electra.

"Such a pretty saddle," said one of the

girls who had ridden her and fallen off. "Too bad she's so hard to ride."

Electra paid them no attention. She kept watching for Alana.

As the other ponies trotted around the field with the royal children, Electra stood alone, watching and waiting.

"Time to dismount, children, class is almost over," instructed their teacher.

Electra let out a sad sigh as the children climbed off the other ponies.

As she plodded back to the barn, her ears perked up. "Electra!" Alana was waving to her from the end of the path.

Electra charged over. "I thought you weren't coming."

"So did I, but then I changed my mind." Alana wheeled her chair towards Electra, and reached up to touch the saddle. "That's beautiful. You designed it?"

"Yes, just for you."

Alana crossed her arms. "You shouldn't have done that."

"Why not?"

"Because I'm not going to take part in the selection ceremony. I don't need a royal pony any more."

Electra's jaw dropped open. "Why not?"

"Well, when you said you're smart enough to know what you can't do, I decided I am, too. I don't want to be queen someday. So I told my parents my younger sister will be next to rule."

Electra stepped back in surprise. "Alana, no! Of course you can rule."

"Then why can't you be a royal pony?" Alana looked angry.

"Because no one can ride me." Electra stomped a hoof. "I thought this saddle might convince you to try one more time."

"It is very beautiful, and I can't believe you had it made for me. But I'm not going to try riding you again. What's the point?" Alana stared off for a few moments. "We can't go very far or very fast. My father and guard would have to walk alongside us. I'd rather just sit in the garden with you and paint if that's all right."

Electra nodded. "Sure it is. Let me return my saddle to the barn, and I'll meet you over there."

While Alana went to the gardens, Electra walked to the barn.

"So, how did your friend like the saddle?" Mulligan asked.

"Oh, she loved it. But she won't ride me. She doesn't even want a royal pet."

"I'm sorry to hear it. You'll find your perfect match."

I already did, but she doesn't want me. "Do you think someday I could work in the barn with you? I really enjoyed designing the saddle."

"Electra, I'm certain you're going to be a wonderful royal pet," Mulligan said. "But yes, if you decide to stay and work at the academy, you could join me in the barn, of course."

Electra nodded and forced a smile. She'd much rather be a royal pet. But working on saddles wouldn't be so bad. She walked towards Alana in the garden.

"I'm going to miss these roses," she said.

"What do you mean?" Electra asked.

"Once the children are done with riding lessons and this semester's training at school, we return to our kingdoms."

Electra nodded and sniffed. "I'll miss you."

"Me too."

Electra used her nose to nudge Alana's shoulder. "Please don't give up your right to be queen."

"I have to."

"No, you don't."

Alana laughed softly. "There are too many things I can't do because of this chair."

"But there are so many wonderful things you can do. Most important, you're smart and kind. You'd be a wonderful ruler. You

belong on a throne."

"I can't even sit on a pony. How can I claim the right to sit on a throne?"

Then the answer hit Electra like a bolt of lightning. She even felt her horn glowing softly again. "Alana, come back tomorrow and I promise, I will prove you wrong."

Chapter Eleven

Electra raced to the riding barn and found Mulligan working on a saddle. "Mulligan, I need your help with my saddle."

He looked confused. "We already made your saddle."

"I need to make some improvements."

Electra explained what she wanted to do, and he smiled. "That's a wonderful idea! It'll take some time."

Electra shook her head. "I need it tomorrow."

Mulligan pushed aside his project. "Then we better get started!"

Electra was exhausted by the time she got to her stall that night.

"What were you doing all day?" Rasha asked.

"The most important thing I'll ever do," she said, before falling fast asleep.

The next morning, Electra waited in the barn until she spotted Alana in the garden. She galloped over. "Come see your new saddle!"

"I don't understand," Alana said, but she followed Electra to the barn. Her father and guard joined them.

"Mulligan, can you please saddle me up?" Electra asked.

The saddle sat propped on a workbench. A high back rose from the seat and two thick straps hung off the side. Alana would be totally supported by the design.

Alana's mouth dropped open as the beautiful saddle floated through the air on to Electra's back, buckling itself onto her. "Think you can sit on that by yourself?"

Alana clapped and squealed in delight. "Yes!"

Electra bent one of her front legs and stretched out the other so she was bowing. "I'd be honoured to ride with you, Your Majesty."

"Oh my gosh, this is perfect!"

Alana's father placed her on top of Electra and fastened the straps. "Are you secure?"

"Yes! You don't need to walk beside us. We'll be OK. Electra, let's ride. Let's go up to the field with the other children."

Electra didn't mind following her command. Slowly, carefully, she walked up to the riding field.

"You can go faster! I'm totally fine up here. I can't believe it!" Alana said.

Electra started trotting and Alana laughed. "I love this!"

They joined the other ponies and children in the middle of their riding lessons.

"You better get off that pony; she's dangerous," said a little girl.

"She's a wild pony!" said another.

"No. She's a perfect pony," Alana said, stroking Electra's mane.

"Why do you have such a strange saddle?" asked a boy.

The other children stared and pointed at it.

"It's not a saddle," said Electra loudly.

"What is it then?" asked a little girl.

"It's a throne fit for a future queen. Alana is too special to ride in a regular saddle."

The children were all quiet.

Prince Dmitri stomped his foot. "I want a saddle throne. I must speak to my father about this immediately."

Alana leaned forward and whispered, "Thank you, Electra. You really are the perfect pony. Let's ride. Fast."

"As you wish!" Electra dashed off through the field while Alana whooped and shouted for joy.

After riding for a long time, they returned to the barn.

"How'd it go?" Alana's father asked.

"It was wonderful! We rode so fast and I didn't have any problems at all. And all the children were jealous of my beautiful saddle," Alana said.

"I think you've found the pony you'll be choosing as your royal pet during the selection ceremony," her father said with a smile.

Alana looked at him with wide eyes. "Oh no, Father. I don't want Electra to be my pet."

·⋆ Chapter Twelve ⋆·

Stunned, Electra ran from the barn.

Alana was shouting something after her, but it didn't matter. Electra had been certain Alana was her perfect match. She knew she could really make a difference for Alana, helping her rule, helping her see her kingdom from her beautiful riding throne.

But Alana didn't want Electra, and there was nothing she could do about that.

Electra ran faster than she'd ever run, but she couldn't outrun her broken heart.

It was still aching in her chest. She tore across the fields, running until she got to the rainbow that led back to the hundred kingdoms. "Oh no! The stairs aren't there!"

Only the headmaster and headmistress could enchant the rainbow to form stairs. Right then, it was just a rainbow. There was no way to leave.

She stood there breathless, uncertain of what to do. How had everything gone so wrong? She'd been so certain she was going to be the best rider in class. But she was the worst. And she'd been so certain Alana would want to choose her, but she didn't.

Soon, she heard a rumble approaching. In the distance, she saw Daisy pulling the chariot. Alana's red hair was shining in the sun.

Electra wished she had Daisy's Glitter

Gift. She really wanted to disappear.

"Electra!" Alana called as the chariot approached. "Wait!"

Electra did not want to hear why Alana didn't want her for a pet. No excuse would make her feel better. Her heart was already hurting too much.

Daisy ran up next to Electra and smiled. "You'll be so lucky to have Alana as your royal match. She's so special."

Electra kicked at the dirt. "She doesn't want me. She said so."

"That's right. I don't want you as a pet," Alana said. "I want you to be my best friend. You're more to me than a pet. I want us to rule *together*."

Electra blinked a few times. "You mean you *will* pick me when we have our selection ceremony?"

"Of course!" Alana laughed. "You're the best pony a girl could ever have. The best friend."

Electra went over to Alana, nuzzling her cheek. "I still have to pass the introductory riding class. I'm not sure if I can."

"Of course you can! Let's get back so you two can catch up on lessons. The final exam is in two days!" Daisy said.

They galloped back to school, and Alana's father helped Alana get out of the chariot and into the saddle again.

"Let's run," Alana told Electra.

Electra started off in a trot, then soon was racing around the track. Alana was whooping with delight from her saddle throne.

They spent the afternoon working on prancing, posing, and galloping. "This feels so easy with you," Electra said.

"We were meant to be together," Alana said, ruffling her mane.

Electra nodded. "I just hope we're ready for the exam."

Chapter Thirteen

One by one, the ponies paired up with a child and followed Professor Wallina's instructions. They raced as fast as they could. Electra was at the head of the pack. They trotted and galloped and jumped low fences. They pranced and they paraded around the track with perfect posture.

While the professor tallied up the exam scores, Electra and Alana visited the rose garden. "I'm sure going to miss you when you go home," Electra said.

"I'll be back to visit. I promise," Alana

said, picking a flower. "But I have to catch up on studying at home, too. I haven't been working very hard to be queen. I need to change that."

"I know you can do it."

"You're right. I can. Thanks for helping me realize that, Electra."

"Thank you for not letting me give up on being a royal pony."

Alana wrapped her arms around Electra's neck, hugging her.

"Let's see if they finished scoring the exams yet." Electra trotted back to the training field.

Professor Wallina stood in front of the crowd. "I have good news, children and ponies. You all passed the final exam. You'll all move on to our more advanced classes next term."

The ponies and children cheered.

"Let's celebrate," Alana said. "What's something special we can do?"

"I know," Electra said. "Do you have your art supplies?"

Alana nodded. "They're with my things in the barn."

"Let's go get them!"

After they retrieved Alana's things, Electra raced through the fields.

"Where are we going?" Alana asked.

"You'll see!" Electra headed towards the trail in the forest.

"We're going to see the seaponies?" Alana asked.

"Yes!"

"Woo-hoo!" shouted Alana.

"You'll have to sing to get them to rise up."

"I can do that."

"We'll run through the orchard so you can grab an apple for Marina. She loves them!" Electra rode towards the orchard, and Alana picked a few apples. Then she trotted through the trail in the forest until they got to the river. "Ready to sing?"

"Yes! I hope this works!" Alana cleared her throat. *"In all the world . . . I'm the luckiest girl . . . because I have such a very good friend."*

Soon, Marina's head bobbed up from underwater.

Alana gasped. "Hello! We brought you an apple!"

"Thank you," Marina whispered.

Electra bowed down so Alana could offer her the apple. "Do you mind if I draw your picture, Marina?"

"That would be lovely."

Alana hummed as she worked. "This is the happiest day of my life, Electra. I'm so excited about all the things we'll do together."

"Me too." Electra lit up her horn and hooves. They glowed stronger and brighter than they ever had before. "We're truly a perfect match."

The magic continues! Turn the page for
a sneak peek at Belissima's story ...

Lisa Ann Scott

Enchanted Pony Academy

Dreams That Sparkle

Chapter One

Belissima took a deep breath and looked around her stall in the Earth barn. She couldn't believe that selection week was actually here! In just a few days, she'd be leaving Enchanted Pony Academy. She *hoped* she'd be leaving – this week the royal children were coming to the Academy to pick a graduating pony as their royal pet. If Belissima was chosen, she'd move to a new kingdom and use her magic to help rule!

For now, she was more nervous than excited. So many emotions were swirling inside of her: excitement, fear, sadness and glee. She'd never felt this way before, not even the day she first climbed the rainbow stairs to join the academy two years ago.

"How are you going to style your mane? It's such a beautiful colour," Skydancer asked, rustling her wings just outside Belissima's stall door.

Belissima flicked her tail. "I'm not doing anything special."

Rose poked her nose in. "Why not?"

"Because she doesn't have to do anything to look amazing. She's already so pretty," Razzle said, joining the group. "Belissima, you're going to be First Pony, I'm sure of it."

"Oh, I don't know about that," Belissima said.

"Of course you're going to be chosen first. You're so gorgeous that everyone will want you for a pet," Razzle said.

Belissima stomped her hoof. "That's not the only reason for children to select their royal pony."

Skydancer nodded. "Right, our Glitter Gifts are important, too." Skydancer was a first-year pegapony who could talk to any other winged creature. It was an amazing and useful gift. She'd been able to communicate with the two young dragons that had landed near their school. Without

Skydancer's Glitter Gift, no one would have known they were looking for help, not trouble.

Belissima frowned. Her Glitter Gift wasn't very exciting. Her coat could change colour and sparkle. Big deal. That had placed her in the pageantry study group. She really loved her healing classes and would've preferred that group instead, but a colour-changing coat had nothing to do with healing. So she'd spent the last two years perfecting different gaits and fancy moves, like riding a figure-eight and walking on her hind legs. She'd worked her hardest in her classes, but pageantry skills weren't her true passion.

Daisy galloped into the stables with a tray levitated by her side. "Happy selection week! We made you a treat! It just came out of the oven. It's posy pie!"

"Oh, thank you," said Belissima. It was

tradition for the first-year students to present gifts to the graduating ponies during selection week. Some ponies put together performances or wrote songs and poems. Belissima thought it was a lovely gesture.

"I found the *Magic Treats and Eats Cookbook* in the library," Daisy said proudly. "It's filled with surprise recipes. All the first-year ponies from Earth barn worked on the pie together. Take a taste and see what happens." Daisy giggled and tried to hide her smile.

"Is this a trick?" Belissima asked.

"A good one," Rose said. "You're going to love it!"

Belissima took a small bite of the fruity pie. As soon as her lips touched the treat, a cloud of flower petals fluttered in the air all around her. "Oh, how wonderful!"

"And your breath will smell like flowers

for a while!" Daisy said.

Belissima laughed, and indeed, she smelled a lovely floral scent.

"There are so many interesting recipes," Daisy said. "The ponies in Water barn made cloud candy. It's cotton candy that floats!"

Razzle frowned. "Stone wanted to make the *atchoo* cookies. The recipe said it would make a pony sneeze for hours!"

"He's nothing but a jokester," said

Skydancer, frowning. "Good thing we found the cookbook first."

"There were other horrible recipes that seemed like pranks, instead of wonderful surprises," Daisy said. "I even saw one that gives you mouldy green spots all over your coat!"

"Oh my!" Belissima said.

"Don't worry, we hid the cookbook in the library where Stone will never find it," Razzle said.

Skydancer giggled. "Behind *The Complete History of the Hundred Kingdoms*. Have you seen the size of that book? He'll never look there."

All the ponies laughed with her.

Electra bounded into the barn with several flower garlands draped over her neck. "Happy selection week! The ponies in Sky barn made one for each of the ponies in the selection ceremony. I saved the prettiest one for you, Belissima, since you're the prettiest pony."

Belissima forced a smile. No one ever mentioned she had the top grades in her class, or that she was a leader who always tried to be patient and pleasant with all the ponies at school. The only thing anyone ever said about Belissima was that she was pretty. Or beautiful. Or gorgeous. She really hoped whichever child chose her could see that she was so much more than her looks.

The prince or princess who would be her perfect match would love to explore fields of flowers and chase butterflies until they fluttered off into the sky. They'd splash through creeks and frolic under waterfalls. Together, they'd creep through spooky forests and collect wild herbs to make healing potions. They'd both get so muddy,

no one would be able to tell what shade
of purple Belissima
was.

But her perfect match would *not* spend time brushing her mane or decorating her hooves. They would not try countless headdresses and accessories on her. They would not waste their time primping and preening. A mirror would not be needed in her stable.

Electra levitated the garland around Belissima's neck.

"Thank you, Electra," she said. "This must have taken a lot of work to create."

"It did. I conjured up a spell to help me weave the flowers."

"Excellent! Keep working hard and your magic will continue to grow," Belissima said.

Electra's horn and hooves suddenly glowed. It was a wonderful Glitter Gift.

"We better go get our seats before the ceremony starts," Skydancer said. "We'll be cheering for you. Just think, in a few days, you'll be leaving the academy with your royal child! I can't wait to meet your perfect match."

Belissima felt panicked realizing how much she'd miss these friends she'd come to love so much. The child who chose her just *had* to be her perfect match. Otherwise, they'd both be so very unhappy.

She raised her chin, determined to put her best hoof forward during selection week. She had to be sure the children could see beyond her pretty coat and fancy mane.

Lisa Ann Scott

is the author of *School of Charm*. A former TV news reporter and anchor, she currently works as a voice-over artist and writer. She lives in Upstate New York with her husband and two kids. For more about Lisa and her books, visit LisaAnnScott.com.

Collect them all ...

Lisa Ann Scott

Enchanted Pony Academy

All That Glitters

Lisa Ann Scott

Enchanted Pony Academy

Wings That Shine

Collect them all ...

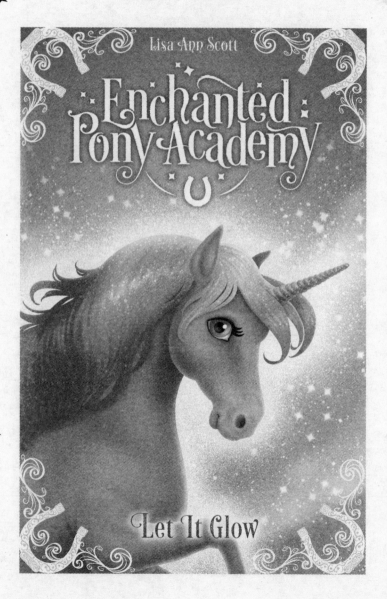

Lisa Ann Scott

Enchanted
Pony Academy

Let It Glow

Collect them all ...

Lisa Ann Scott

Enchanted Pony Academy

Dreams That Sparkle